Professor Possum's
Great Adventure

Written by Michael Pellowski
Illustrated by Julie Durrell

Troll Associates

Library of Congress Cataloging-in-Publication Data

Pellowski, Michael.
    Professor Possum's great adventure.

    (Fiddlesticks)
    Summary: Professor Possum, adventurer and master
butterfly collector, mounts an expedition to capture
the rare species known as regal patriarch and finds
danger on a jungle island.
    [1. Jungles—Fiction.   2. Butterflies—Fiction.
3. Adventure and adventurers—Fiction.   4. Opossums
—Fiction]   I. Durrell, Julie, ill.   II. Title.
III. Series.
PZ7.P3656Pr   1989   [E]   88-1281
ISBN 0-8167-1341-3 (lib. bdg.)
ISBN 0-8167-1342-1 (pbk.)

Professor Phineas O. Possum hunched over his desk and stared at the old, crumbling sheet of paper before him. The professor smiled in a satisfied way. What a find the map was! It was the only one of its kind in the entire world.

Professor Possum had chanced upon the map after a treasure-hunting trip to Africa. Phineas had stopped in Egypt on his way home. There he had discovered the chart in a tiny, dusty old shop.

The shop's owner thought the map was a useless chart to an island that did not exist. Phineas O. Possum knew better. He gladly paid a tidy sum for it.

Such things were no mystery to the professor. He was a world-famous adventurer and explorer. He was also a leading expert in the study of butterflies of all kinds.

4

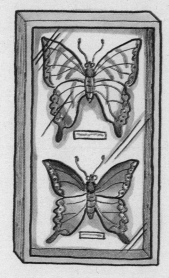

The world's largest and most complete
collection of butterflies belonged to the
professor. The showcases in his study were
filled with all sorts of beautiful butterflies.

He had a zebra butterfly and a tiger
swallowtail. He had a dogface butterfly and
a pygmy blue. Of course, there were
monarchs and viceroys, too.

But there was one butterfly Professor Possum did not have. That butterfly was the mysterious regal patriarch.

"Phineas, do you think the regal patriarch really exists?" asked Dr. Bandicoot.

Dr. Bandicoot was a close friend of the professor's. He, too, was an expert on butterflies.

"No one has seen a regal patriarch in hundreds of years," Dr. Bandicoot continued.

Phineas Possum looked up from the map
he was studying. He smiled at his friend.
"Everyone thought Danger Island and Mount
Flower Pollen did not exist either," Phineas
said to Dr. Bandicoot. "But now I have a
map to the island and its mountain peak. If
regal patriarchs do exist, *that* is where I'll
find them. And when I do, I'll bring one
home for my collection."

The next day, Dr. Bandicoot helped
Professor Possum prepare for his great
adventure.

While Dr. Bandicoot packed food,
Phineas dressed for the journey. He put on
his boots and his lucky leather jacket. Over
one shoulder, he slipped a pouch for the
map. Over the other, he coiled a length of
strong rope for mountain climbing. Finally,
he added the finishing touch, the old jungle
hat he always wore on his adventures.

"Time to go," announced the professor, picking up his trusty butterfly net. He went into the next room where his friend was waiting.

"Here is your backpack," Dr. Bandicoot said. "You're all ready." Inside the pack were supplies and the things the professor used for collecting butterflies.

Dr. Bandicoot drove Professor Possum to the airfield where Phineas kept his private plane. The aircraft was ready for takeoff.

Professor Possum and Dr. Bandicoot loaded the gear into the airplane. Then Phineas and Bandicoot shook hands. The professor climbed into the plane and got behind the controls. Carefully, he checked the gauges and dials. Everything was in perfect order. Phineas Possum started the engines.

"Good luck and good butterfly hunting,"
called Dr. Bandicoot, as the airplane began
to move. Professor Possum smiled and waved.
Away the plane sped down the runway.
It lifted off the ground and soared into
the clouds. The adventure had begun.

Using the map, Phineas Possum flew the plane in the direction of the strange and mysterious Danger Island.

He flew over tall mountain ranges with snow-tipped peaks. He flew across endless stretches of churning, blue ocean. On and on the plane flew.

The aircraft continued, passing dozens of tiny islands below. The professor carefully noted each one on the map before moving on. Finally, after what seemed like endless hours of flying, Phineas O. Possum neared his goal.

"According to the map, Danger Island has to be down there somewhere," Phineas said, as he searched among many small islands below. "But where? Where is that island?"

Suddenly, Phineas spied a glimmering emerald dot below. The plane dropped out of the clouds as Phineas circled for a closer look.

Slowly, a grin spread across the professor's face. On the island below he had sighted the majestic peak of Mount Flower Pollen.

"That's it! Danger Island," he exclaimed happily. "I've found the home of the rare regal patriarch."

Lower, lower, lower went the plane, as
Phineas flew along the shore in search of a
safe landing place. At last he spotted a long
stretch of sandy, white beach. It was perfect.

"Danger Island, here I come," the professor
said. And he brought the plane in for a perfect
landing.

Once on the island, the professor wasted little time. He climbed out of the plane and removed his gear. Soon he was ready to travel.

Phineas adjusted the pack on his back and fastened his butterfly net to it. He held the coiled rope in his hand and looked over the strange island. He'd never seen anything like it before. At the edge of the beach was a dense jungle. Phineas shrugged his shoulders and boldly started off toward it.

The jungle of Danger Island might have chilled the blood of some—but not Professor Phineas O. Possum. The growls of fierce jungle animals did not worry him. When he heard the hissing noise of a steaming swamp, he was not frightened.

The brave professor had only one thought in his mind. He thought about the distant slopes of Mount Flower Pollen. There, he hoped he would find the rare butterfly no one had seen in hundreds of years. Step by step, he marched through the dark and spooky jungle.

19

Above, strange-looking birds twittered loudly as Professor Possum fought his way through the thick tangle of branches. Monkeys in treetops chattered. Eerie sounds filled the air.

But did Professor Possum care? No! Phineas whistled a merry tune as he carved a path through the bush.

Then at long last, the jungle parted to reveal a wide river. "This is a bit of a problem," Phineas said. He stopped and eyed the dark, murky water.

What was the problem? The river was overflowing with big, hungry crocodiles. Their heads bobbed above the water like hundreds of living logs.

Phineas stepped closer to the water. A crocodile opened its huge mouth to reveal rows of long, sharp teeth. The professor stepped back just as the jaws snapped shut. It was a narrow escape.

"Hmmm," thought the professor, "crossing this river without becoming crocodile chow won't be easy."

The professor stared at the crocodiles.
Their heads reminded him of steppingstones.
"Steppingstones!" his voice rang out.
"That's it!"

Phineas O. Possum was one of the best
hopscotch players anywhere. With a little
luck he could get across with a triple
hop-skip-and-a-jump.

Phineas waited until the crocodile heads were lined up just right. Then he got a good running start. "Here I go," he shouted, as he sped toward the water.

Hop! He touched one head. Skip! He bounded away before the crocodile could snap at him. Jump! He landed on another. And so it went until he was safely across.

"Phew!" sighed the professor as he wiped his brow. "That was hard work, but it was kind of fun." He laughed and walked off into the jungle.

A short time later, Professor Possum
entered a large clearing. In the clearing he
came face to face with another problem.
It was a furry, striped problem with fangs
and claws.

Phineas stopped in his tracks. "A tiger,"
he said. "And a mean-looking one at that!"

"*Growll,*" the tiger snarled. But Phineas
paid no attention to the uproar. Instead, he
tuned his hearing to a faint buzzing sound
above his head. Looking up, he spied a
beehive dangling from a tree.

"That gives me an idea," he said.

The tiger prepared to charge. Calmly, Phineas removed the butterfly net from his pack. Turning it around, he used the handle to pry off the bees' nest. It dropped gently to the ground before him.

The tiger roared one last time and ran
toward Phineas. What a frightful sight!
   Phineas had only seconds to act. In one
quick motion, he grabbed the nest and
kicked it toward the tiger. His aim was right
on target.

Pop!

The beehive hit the tiger on the head and burst apart. Angry bees started to fly around the big cat.

Buzz! Buzz! Buzz!

"*Yowll*," howled the tiger, as the mad bees began to sting. The tiger turned and darted off into the jungle, with the bees following close behind.

"Touchdown!" Phineas chuckled, as he put the butterfly net back in his pack.

But Professor Possum wasn't out of danger yet. When he reached the other side of the clearing, he walked right into *more* trouble.

Sploosh!

Into a pit of quicksand he fell. Quickly, Professor Possum began to sink. Down, down, down he went.

But Phineas O. Possum wasn't the type to panic. Keeping one arm above water, he uncoiled his rope. He knotted a loop in one end.

With one mighty throw he tossed the loop over the top of a nearby tree and pulled it tight.

Then Phineas began to pull with all of his strength. The sapling began to bend. When it refused to bend anymore, Phineas felt the grip of the quicksand begin to loosen.

"Here I go," he shouted.

Whoosh! Out of the quicksand shot the professor. The bent sapling straightened itself and hurled Phineas into the air like a rocket. High above the treetops he sailed.

As luck would have it, Phineas came
down right on the back of an elephant. What
a surprise! The startled beast trumpeted and
thundered off into the jungle.

Phineas held on tight. The elephant was
running right toward Mount Flower Pollen.
So Phineas stayed aboard and got a free ride.
But what a wild ride it was!

Finally, at the foot of Mount Flower Pollen, the professor decided it was time to get off.

Reaching up, he grabbed a tree limb. Away ran the elephant, leaving Phineas dangling in space. "Thanks for the lift," called the professor, as the elephant disappeared into the jungle.

Professor Possum dropped to the ground. He adjusted his pack and started up the side of the mountain. Higher, higher, higher he went.

At long last, he reached a grassy meadow on a sunny slope. All around were strange plants and beautiful flowers. "I've never seen anything like this anywhere," Phineas said.

He took a closer look. The strange plants
were tiny, little trees no higher than flowers.
And the flowers! There were red flowers
with blue centers and pink flowers with
purple petals. There were big flowers and
little flowers. Sweet-smelling flowers were
everywhere.

Phineas walked out into the middle of the meadow. Suddenly, flocks of beautiful butterflies rose up out of the flowers and plants. Professor Possum couldn't believe his eyes.

"Regal patriarchs!" he said in amazement. "Hundreds of them! Thousands of them!"

For a moment, Phineas just stood and stared at the beautiful sight. At last, he dropped his backpack and picked up his butterfly net.

Off he raced to catch the biggest, most beautiful regal patriarch of all.

Around and around the meadow, the butterfly flew. Right behind it ran Professor Possum with his net held high.

"Now!" shouted Phineas. With one mighty swoop, he captured the rare and beautiful creature. Proudly, he held up his prize.

Professor Possum carefully carried the butterfly back to his pack. He took out a glass jar in which to put it.

The professor looked at the butterfly. He looked at the jar. Suddenly, he felt very sad.

"I can't do it," he said. Leaning close to the regal patriarch, he whispered, "You belong outside in a beautiful meadow. I just can't put you in that jar."

With a smile on his face, Professor
Possum opened the net and turned the
butterfly loose. It flitted around his head as
if thanking him, and then it flew away.

"Good-bye, butterfly," Phineas called.
Professor Possum sighed and looked at the
meadow. The flowers and tiny trees gave
him an idea.

"These would look great in my back yard," he cried. "I'll dig some up and take them home with me. That way, the trip won't be a total loss."

Professor Possum took as many different trees and flowers as he could carry. He climbed down the mountain and hiked back through the jungle. He loaded everything onto his plane and took off. Little did the professor know there was something very special about those little trees he had taken.

After arriving home, Professor Possum planted the tiny trees and beautiful flowers in his garden. After several weeks, the plants and flowers began to bud and bloom. Soon the professor's garden was as beautiful as the slopes of Mount Flower Pollen.

It was then that Phineas invited Dr. Bandicoot over to hear the story of his greatest adventure.

"So tell me, Phineas," asked
Dr. Bandicoot, "is there really a regal
patriarch?"

"Follow me," Professor Possum replied.
He led Dr. Bandicoot into the new garden.

"My word!" cried the doctor in surprise.
Fluttering from flower to flower were dozens
of beautiful regal patriarchs. "How?"
Bandicoot sputtered.

"I brought back many strange plants and flowers from Danger Island," Phineas explained. "I didn't know it, but on the branches of the tiny trees were butterfly eggs. In a few weeks, the eggs hatched into caterpillars. And the caterpillars turned into butterflies. The butterflies were regal patriarchs. My flower garden is their new home."

Bandicoot patted the professor on the back. "Phineas O. Possum," he said, "you've done it again."

The professor just looked at the beautiful butterflies and smiled.